When Aristotle was a kitten, he did not know that cats have nine lives. His mother knew, of course. But I'm not going to tell him, she thought. Already he's a tearaway, much bolder than his brothers and sisters, and if he knows that he's got nine lives to play with, he'll take all sorts of risks.

7

So she didn't say anything to Aristotle except "Goodbye" when he left home and went to live with an old lady.

A strange looking old lady she was, with a beaky nose and a chin that jutted out, and she wore black clothes and a tall black hat on top of her stringy grey hair.

Her name was Bella Donna, and it was she who decided to call her new kitten Aristotle.

"Really," she said, "I ought to have a black cat, but it'll be a nice change to have a white one."

Aristotle

DICK KING-SMITH

illustrated by BOB GRAHAM

WALKER BOOKS

For Zona ~ D.K-S.

To Caitlin and her coven ~ B.G.

First published 2003 by Walker Books Ltd
87 Vauxhall Walk, London SE11 5HJ

2 4 6 8 10 9 7 5 3 1

Text © 2003 Foxbusters Ltd
Illustrations © 2003 Bob Graham

The right of Dick King–Smith and Bob Graham to be identified as
author and illustrator respectively of this work has been asserted by them in
accordance with the Copyright, Designs and Patents Act 1988

This book has been typeset in M Bembo

Printed in China

British Library Cataloguing in Publication Data:
a catalogue record for this book
is available from the British Library

ISBN 0-7445-8320-9

But the very first day that Aristotle went to live in Bella Donna's funny old cottage, he decided he would explore it from top to bottom. Or rather from bottom to top, because when he'd looked all round the downstairs rooms and then the upstairs rooms, he thought he'd like to get up on the roof.

It was a thatched roof, so that, once Aristotle climbed up the creeper that grew on the walls of the cottage, he could easily walk up the thatch to the single chimney.

Then, because he was curious, as all cats are, he scrambled up the chimney-stack and looked down the chimney-pot and wondered what the hole in it was for.

At that very moment a big puff of smoke came up, right in Aristotle's face, which made him cough and sneeze and lose his balance, and down the chimney he fell.

Bella Donna had just lit her kitchen fire when down into the fireplace came a great load of soot, which put out the flames, and after the soot, a kitten that had been white but was now black as a witch's hat.

"Well, my boy," said Bella Donna, "that's the first of your nine lives gone. Good job the chimney was so dirty or you'd have burned to death. You'd better be a bit more careful, Aristotle, if you want to grow to be a cat. Only eight to go."

There was a fair old bit of tidying up to do after that. Using a large broomstick that stood in a corner of her kitchen, Bella Donna swept up all the mess that the fall of soot had made. Then she laid the fire again and lit it. Then she heated some water on it, which, when warm enough, she poured into a big tin basin. Then she picked up Aristotle and put him in the basin and rinsed him and soaped him and rinsed him again.

Aristotle had mixed feelings about all this. On the one hand, like all cats, he hated being dirty and it was lovely to be a white kitten

again. On the other, he hated water. But once
Bella Donna had rubbed him dry and set
before him a dish of meat, he decided that his
new owner meant him more good than harm.

Aristotle did not know what the meat
was (it was in fact a mixture of frogs' legs,
snails and fried woodlice), but he thought it
was delicious. He cleared the dish, lay down
in front of the fire and fell fast asleep.

When he woke up again it was to find
himself alone. The old lady had gone,
shutting the kitchen door behind her, and so,
he noticed, had her broomstick.

Where she had gone he did not know,
but what with the big meal he had eaten and
the heat of the fire, Aristotle began to feel

very thirsty. He set off to explore the kitchen

for something to drink.

On a table, his eyes told him, stood a large

heavy earthenware jug. He jumped up and

peered into it. It was, his nose told him, full

of milk of some sort, though from which

animal he did not know (it was in fact a

mixture of cow's milk, goat's milk and ewe's milk, with a dash of pigeon's milk added).

He put a paw down into the jug and stirred the liquid around, which, his ears told him, made an appetizing sloshy sound. He pulled out the paw and licked it and his tongue told him that it tasted delightful.

Eagerly Aristotle put both paws on the rim of the jug and shoved his head down inside it and began greedily to drink. As the level of the milk dropped, so he pushed more of himself into the heavy jug, until at last it tipped over on top of him.

When, just after midnight, Bella Donna came back, she opened the kitchen door, propped her broomstick in the corner and then heard a most melancholy mewing.

By the dying light of the fire, she could see that her great earthenware milk jug was standing upside down in the middle of the kitchen table, that there was milk all over both table and floor, and that the noise was coming from inside the upturned jug.

Lighting a candle, she lifted the jug to reveal beneath it a whiter than white, wetter than wet, woebegone kitten.

Once more she warmed water to wash
Aristotle. Once more she rubbed him dry.
Once more she addressed him.

"Well, my boy," said Bella Donna,
"that's the second of your lives gone. Good

job the jug tipped over or you'd have stuck in it, head down, and drowned. You'd better be a bit more careful, Aristotle, or you'll never make old bones. Only seven lives to go."

Dry and warm now, the white kitten looked up at the black-clothed old woman and felt strangely comforted by the sound of her voice.

Before she went to bed, Bella put Aristotle out in the garden.

"I expect you drank a lot of that milk,"

she said to him, "and there's been enough mess in the kitchen without you adding to it." What a rascal he is, she said to herself. He only came here yesterday but already he's used up two lives. At this rate, he'll never grow into a proper witch's cat.

But in fact Aristotle managed to keep out of trouble for quite a while. A whole week went by and the white kitten behaved sensibly. He ate his meat and drank his milk and didn't scratch at the curtains or the chair covers and didn't make any messes in the cottage.

Indeed, by the end
of that week Bella
Donna had trained
him to use a dirt tray.

"You didn't make a very good start,
Aristotle," she said to him, "but now
you're doing fine. Just keep on keeping
out of mischief." And she crossed her
long knobbly fingers.

If Aristotle had gone to an ordinary home
things might have been different, but Bella's
old cottage was in many ways a risky sort of
place for an adventurous kitten.

It stood in the middle of a little wood in
which were many tall trees, and through
which flowed a swift steep-banked stream.
On one side of the wood there was a twisty
road, and on the other a lofty embankment
along the top of which ran a railway line.
There was also a farm nearby, on which lived
a large dog.

Aristotle's next adventure took place up a tall tree. Climbing was something he found he rather liked, and he often now scrambled up the creeper on the cottage walls and up the thatched roof to sit upon the ridge-pole at the top (though he kept away from the chimney-pot). He enjoyed this lofty perch but the cottage was quite a low building and the trees around it were, he could see, much higher.

So one fine morning, Aristotle chose a tall
tree and leapt up its trunk onto the lowest
branch, and then onto a higher one, and
so on, up and up, feeling such a clever cat.

But the further up he went, the
thinner and more springy
the branches became, till
at last he found himself

right at the top, clinging
to a thin bough that danced in
the breeze, and he suddenly felt ever
such a scared kitten. The ground, he
could see, was an awful long way down, and
the wind seemed to be getting stronger and
the bough bouncier. He lost his nerve, and his
grip, gave a loud yowl of fright and fell.

By good
fortune, Bella Donna was
looking out of her open
kitchen window and heard
her kitten's cries and saw
him fall, paws spread wide,
tail whirling madly round
and round, down, down,
down, bumping off the
branches as he went.

Let's hope he lands
in the stream, she
thought, and she grabbed

her broomstick and
hurried out.

Luck was on Aristotle's
side, for he did indeed
land, with a great splash, in
water that was very cold
and running very fast. He
swallowed a lot of it as he
struggled and spluttered
and tried in vain to
scramble up the stream's
steep bank. But as he was
swept along, he suddenly

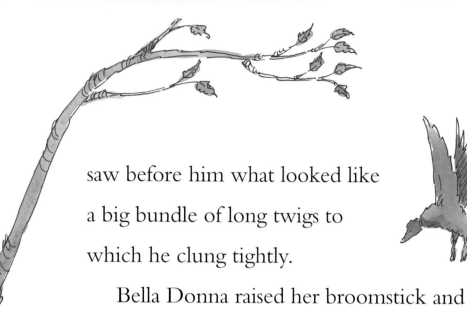

saw before him what looked like
a big bundle of long twigs to
which he clung tightly.

Bella Donna raised her broomstick and
lifted her wet white kitten out.

Aristotle was so out of breath that he
could only manage a feeble mew. He clung

as tightly to Bella Donna as he had to her broomstick, while she cuddled him close to make him feel safe again.

"Well, my boy," she said to him after she'd carried him home and rubbed him down, "you've managed to get through two lives in one go. The fall should have broken your little neck and the stream should have filled your little lungs. It looks as though it'll need a bit of magic to keep you in the land of the living. You really must take more care, Aristotle. Only five lives left now."

Now time passed –
quite a lot of time –
without Aristotle getting into hot water, or
cold water for that matter, or falling out of
trees or down chimneys or into milk jugs, as
he grew from kitten to cat.

Someone less wise than Bella Donna
might have thought that he was over the
worst of his troubles, but though
Bella might have been old
and skinny and ugly,
she was also very
wise indeed. She

knew, in her wisdom, that her white cat would surely have other lives to lose, and so she kept a close eye on him.

Aristotle had grown used to the fact that Bella was mostly around the place by day and that usually she went out at night, leaving him snoozing by the kitchen fire. Being a sharp-eyed animal, he also noticed that she never went out into the darkness without her broomstick, though he did not know why.

By day, Bella Donna was a busy person, so that, try as she would, there were times when the eye she kept on Aristotle was not as close as it should have been.

For example, she often seemed to be heating something – Aristotle did not know what – in a large black cauldron that hung suspended over the kitchen fire. Whatever was in this cauldron needed a lot of stirring, and one day, while Bella was busy at this, Aristotle slipped out for a walk.

For some time he had been curious – as all cats are – about a lot of loud noises that came, now and again, from one side of the wood. There were clanking noises and puffing noises and sometimes a shrill whistle, and they got louder and louder as whatever–it–was drew nearer, and then quieter and quieter as whatever–it–was went away.

On this particular day, what with the crackling of the fire and the bubbling of the liquid in the cauldron, Bella did not hear the clanking and the puffing, but the whistle, when it came, was very loud and very shrill. She looked quickly round the kitchen for Aristotle but there was no sign of him.

Had anyone been watching, they would have been amazed at how swiftly Bella now acted. First she dropped her ladle into the cauldron. Then she lifted the cauldron off the fire. Then she picked up her broomstick from the corner and dashed out.

It had taken Aristotle a good five minutes to get from the cottage and up the embankment

to the railway line, but Bella positively
flew there in no time at all – to see a
terrifying sight.

On the railway track a white cat was walking, sniffing curiously at the steel lines on either side of him, unaware that behind him an old steam train was coming into view, puffing and clanking and now, at sight of the cat, whistling like mad.

Like a lot of white cats, Aristotle was a bit deaf, and he didn't take notice of the noise until the engine was nearly upon him, but then he heard Bella's voice.

"Lie down, Aristotle!" she screeched. "Lie down flat and don't move a whisker!"

Never did Aristotle forget the terrible

noise as the puffing whistling engine and
its clanking rattling coaches passed right
over him, only inches above, it seemed,
as he lay between the rails.

(Never, what's more, did he ever go on the railway track again.)

As the noise died away, he opened his eyes which, in his terror, he had kept tight shut, to see Bella Donna leaning on her broomstick by the edge of the track, and he ran to her and began to rub himself against her legs.

"Well, my boy," she said to him, "that was a near thing, wasn't it? Good job you stayed still like I told you. You want to watch out, Aristotle. Only four lives to go now." And she gave him a long look with her beady eyes.

At the lower end of Bella Donna's wood there was a farm, to which Bella went to buy milk and eggs. Behind the farmhouse was a yard, and in the middle of the yard there stood a big wooden dog kennel. Now that Aristotle was nearly full grown, he often walked down to the farm behind Bella, his white tail waving.

The first time he went there, she stopped at the yard gate and pointed to the kennel.

"Don't go near that," she said to him, "or you'll be sorry. You wait here while I go and see the farmer's wife."

On the next few visits, Aristotle did indeed sit by the gate, staring at the dark opening in the kennel until, one day, he thought he'd like to have a look inside it, and he set off across the yard.

As he got near, he smelt a strange smell coming from it, a smell that he'd never come across before and didn't much like, and then, when he was very close, he heard a noise. It was the noise of someone snoring.

Curious, as all cats are, Aristotle poked his head round the edge of the kennel door and peered into the blackness of the interior. There, fast asleep, lying on its stomach, its great head upon its paws, lay a very large animal – the cause of the smell and the snores.

It so happened that Aristotle had never before in his life seen a dog, and did not know that most dogs don't much like cats. But the smell of this animal was now so strong in his nose and its snoring so loud in his ears that he thought he'd leave it in peace, especially as each snore drew back the creature's lips to show a battery of sharp-looking teeth.

Just as well, for this was not only a large dog but a very fierce dog, which the farmer kept to guard his farmyard. Round its thick neck was a heavy studded leather collar and, attached to this collar at one end and to a ring-bolt in the kennel at the other, was a length of stout chain.

Little did Aristotle dream that this chain would soon save him from losing the last four of his lives in one fell swoop.

For the next couple of visits to the farm with Bella, Aristotle contented himself with just sitting and staring at the smell-filled snore-loud kennel. But then, one day, he decided that, while Bella was buying her eggs and milk, he must just have another peep at the strange animal.

As before, he peered into the darkness within. As before, he saw the great sleeping shape. But then something very unfortunate

happened. Maybe it was the dust from the
dog's straw bedding, maybe it was to do
with the smell of the creature, but suddenly
Aristotle sneezed.

Afterwards he could never clearly
remember what happened next, but Bella
Donna, coming out of the farmhouse carrying
a jug of milk and a basket of eggs, dropped
the lot at the sight which met her eyes.

With a volley of bloodcurdling growls, the big dog came hurtling out of its kennel, inches behind a wildly-fleeing white cat which it overtook and grabbed in its huge jaws.

But the dog's rush took it to the end of
its length of chain. Suddenly brought up
short, its head was jerked back, forcing its
jaws open, and out of them fell a
bewildered befuddled bedraggled Aristotle.

Back in the cottage, once Bella Donna had cleaned him up and satisfied herself that there were no bones broken, she addressed him in stern fashion.

"Well, my boy," she said, "you should have listened to me, shouldn't you? That was a close shave. You want to watch your step, Aristotle. Only three lives to go."

She held him up before her face and looked into his pale eyes. Gazing back into her dark twinkling ones, Aristotle forgot his fright and snuggled thankfully against his friend.

Aristotle never went into the farmyard now. He would walk part of the way with Bella when she went to buy milk and eggs, but at the edge of the wood he'd stop and wait until she came back again.

Sometimes he would hear the barking of that awful monster that lived in the kennel but he had no wish ever to see it again.

Then one day, months later, he did.

Bella was crossing the yard on her way to the farmhouse when she saw the farmer go to the kennel and unclip the chain from the dog's collar. It then lumbered towards her, not in a threatening way but with flattened ears, a wagging tail and a sort of silly grin on its great face.

"Funny thing," the farmer said to her. "Old Gripper, he's a devil with most people – bite 'em as soon as look at 'em, he will – but he seems to like you."

"I expect," said Bella, "that that's because he knows I'm not scared of him." And she put out a hand to the dog and he slobbered over it.

"I'm letting him have a little run round this morning," the farmer said. "There's some boys been scrumping apples out of my orchard. Old Gripper'll soon see them off."

For a while the dog sniffed about among the apple trees and then, making the most of the unaccustomed freedom, went towards the wood, his mind on rabbits.

But it was not a rabbit that saw him coming. It was a white cat.

At sight of the dog, Aristotle forgot all about waiting for Bella and took to his heels. Made silly by fright, he did not run back to the cottage but simply set off through the trees as fast as he could, without thinking where he was going. Seeing the railway embankment on one side and not wishing to go there again, he turned in the opposite direction, making, though he did not know it, straight for the road that ran along the other side of the wood.

Another thing he did not know was that he was being followed.

White is not the best colour for an animal that wants to conceal itself among the greens and browns of woodland, and it was a flash of white that caught Gripper's eye as he left the orchard. Breaking into a lumbering run, he

came to the spot where he had sighted the cat.
It was nowhere to be seen, but the dog put
down his nose and began to follow the scent.
Someone else was following him.

Bella Donna was coming back through
the farmyard with her purchases when she
saw the dog at about the spot on the wood's
edge where she had left her cat. Quickly she
shoved the milk jug and the egg basket under
a bush and grasped her broomstick.

Aristotle meanwhile had reached the twisty road that ran beside the wood. Thinking that he had outpaced the awful monster and so feeling less scared, he stopped to get his breath. But then he looked up the road to see another monster coming – a large lorry.

As he turned to get away from the nasty noisy thing, he came face to face with Gripper, who had been running silently on his trail and now dashed at him, open-mouthed.

"Never seen anything like it in my life before," the lorry driver told his wife later. "There's this white cat, runs clean under my lorry, between the wheels and out the other side, and then there's this big dog, been chasing the cat, and he tries to follow, and I bangs on my brakes, and then suddenly there's this old woman, appears from nowhere, she does, and she's carrying what looks like a broomstick,

and she gives the dog a great
whack with it, and he lets out a howl and runs
back into the wood, and I gets out and there's
no sign of any of 'em, cat, dog, old woman,
all disappeared."

"She had a broomstick, you say?" asked the lorry driver's wife.

"Yes."

"Go on with you! Next thing, you'll be telling me she was all dressed in black, with a tall black hat on her head!"

"She was."

Once he had got over his double fright of being chased by one monster and almost squashed by another, Aristotle managed somehow to make his way home to the cottage, to find Bella Donna at the kitchen fire, stirring something in the cauldron. On

the table stood a jug of milk and a
basket of eggs. In the corner stood her
broomstick.

He ran to her and began to rub himself
madly against her black-stockinged legs,
purring like a steam engine.

"Well, my boy," said Bella Donna, "that was a narrow squeak. I think we have to count that as two lives. Dog or lorry – either would have killed you, Aristotle. So really, out of your nine lives, you've used up eight now. Your ninth life is going to have to last you a long, long time."

She picked up her white cat and stroked him thoughtfully.

"And I'll tell you something, Aristotle," she said to him, "I shouldn't be at all surprised now if it did."

When Bella Donna next went down to the farm, leaving Aristotle behind of course, she went straight to the dog kennel in the yard.

Gripper came out with a rush, only to pull himself to a halt before the chain did, once he saw who it was. Bella tickled him behind his ears and he wagged his tail madly.

"I've come to say I'm sorry," Bella

told him. "I shouldn't have whacked you

with my broomstick. Mind you, if I hadn't,

you'd have run under the lorry. But I

must have hurt your feelings as well as

your bottom. Will you forgive me?"

For answer, the big dog grinned at her
and licked her hand.

Now not just the months but the years
passed, and Aristotle grew into a fine cat
and a sensible cat what's more. He didn't
get into any scrapes and, as Bella had
foreseen, he kept healthy and stayed safe,
happy in his long ninth life.

Dogs, however, have only one life, and
down at the farm Gripper had grown very
old. No longer did he rush out of his
kennel at the approach of strangers. No
longer did he try to bite anyone and

everyone. Mostly he lay in the yard at the end of his chain, thinking of days gone by.

One warm night he lay there, still, in the light of a full moon, and had the strangest of dreams.

In this dream he heard a swishing noise in the sky above and, raising his heavy head, looked up to see a dark shape flying across the face of the moon. It seemed to be riding on something, this dark shape did, and to have on its head a tall black hat. Sitting perched on its shoulder was a white shape, a shape that reminded Old

Gripper of something that had happened years ago. He gave one last great growl before his head dropped upon his paws, never to be raised again.

Strangely, when Bella next went down to the farm, Aristotle followed her as of old, white tail waving. He followed her right into the yard and right past the dark mouth of the kennel. Stretched out from its door, the long chain lay on the ground and at the end of it was the heavy studded dog-collar, unbuckled.

I expect you're wondering if Aristotle is still enjoying his ninth life? Well he is, I can tell you, because he's now not only a grown-up cat but he's a proper witch's cat too, helping the good witch Bella Donna with her work. Some of the strange mixtures that Bella heats in her cauldron each day are food for her and for her cat. But many are magic potions for curing ailments, such as headaches or toothaches or tummyaches.

At night Bella climbs on her broomstick and flies off – Aristotle knows this because he goes with her – carrying these medicines to the homes of sick children, where she gives a spoonful of this or that to the child as it sleeps. Afterwards she always makes sure that she and her cat are home by midnight.

Aristotle's quite an old fellow now, of course, and Bella Donna is an old old woman. Her grey hair is as white as the fur of her cat.

But they're still living happily together
in the old thatched cottage in the wood.
Bella Donna and Aristotle have still
got a lot of time to enjoy one
another's company.